Harrison

A Forest Is Reborn

A Forest Is Reborn

by James R. Newton

Illustrated by Susan Bonners

Thomas Y. Crowell   New York

For two great aunts:
Nora Ellis
Florence Kruetz

Printed in the United States of America.
No part of this book may be used
or reproduced in any manner
whatsoever without written permission
except in the case of brief quotations
embodied in critical articles and reviews.
For information address Thomas Y. Crowell Junior Books,
10 East 53rd Street,
New York, N.Y. 10022.
Published simultaneously in Canada
by Fitzhenry & Whiteside Limited, Toronto.
Designed by Ellen Weiss
Library of Congress Cataloging in Publication Data
Newton, James R.
   A forest is reborn.
   Summary: Describes how a forest renews itself through
a process called plant succession after a destructive
fire.
   1. Forest ecology—Juvenile literature. 2. Forest
reproduction—Juvenile literature. 3. Plant succession—
Juvenile literature. [1. Forest ecology 2. Plant
succession. 3. Forest fires. 4. Ecology]   I. Bonners,
Susan, ill.   II. Title.
QK938.F6N48 1982   581.5'2642   81-43882
ISBN 0-690-04231-0   AACR2
ISBN 0-690-04232-9 (lib. bdg.)

1 2 3 4 5 6 7 8 9 10

First Edition

The jagged spear of lightning streaked down from
the stormy sky. It split the old dead tree apart and
set both halves on fire.

Flames danced away in all directions.
They licked at the leaves and broken branches
that littered the forest floor. They swept up the
trunks of big trees and leaped from branch to branch.
Exploding trees shot out bullets of fire.

The air was filled with crackling noises and the
strong, smoky smell of the burning forest.

2

For several days the fire raged through the
woods. The summer sky turned a dull, hazy gray.
Forest animals fled the heat and smoke.

   People battled the blaze from all directions.
Low-flying airplanes dropped chemicals on the racing
flames. Helicopters doused parts of the fire with
thousands of gallons of water.

   On the ground, fire fighters with bulldozers,
chain saws, and axes cut a wide path around the fire.
They cleared the path of everything that would burn.
Then with shovels and water tanks they fought to
keep the blaze inside this fire line.

    Finally, the forest fire was brought under control and then put out. When the last puff of smoke faded away, only blackened trunks and charred stumps remained. The tall trees were stripped of their branches. Gone were the bushes, shrubs, and vines. In just a few days the forest that had taken centuries to grow was destroyed.

But the land would not stay
this way forever. Gradually, life
would return. Different kinds of plants
would come and go in turn, in a process
called "plant succession."

Each new kind would flourish
as long as it had the amount of
sunshine and shade it needed for
growth. When taller plants around it
blocked out the sunlight, then it
would die and a new kind of plant—
one that could thrive in a shadier
environment—would take its place.

Finally, a new forest
would stand where the old one
used to be.

9

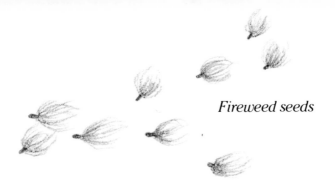

Fireweed seeds

Fireweed

A few weeks after the fire, purple and green patches of fireweeds spring up from the ashes. Their seeds, dangling beneath silken parachutes, had floated into the burned area from the surrounding woods. Winds also bring the seeds of grasses and other narrow-leaved plants, which quickly sprout and add their color to the blackened land. These are the sun-loving plants. They are the first to grow in the nearly shadeless burned-over area because they do not need to be protected from the sun.

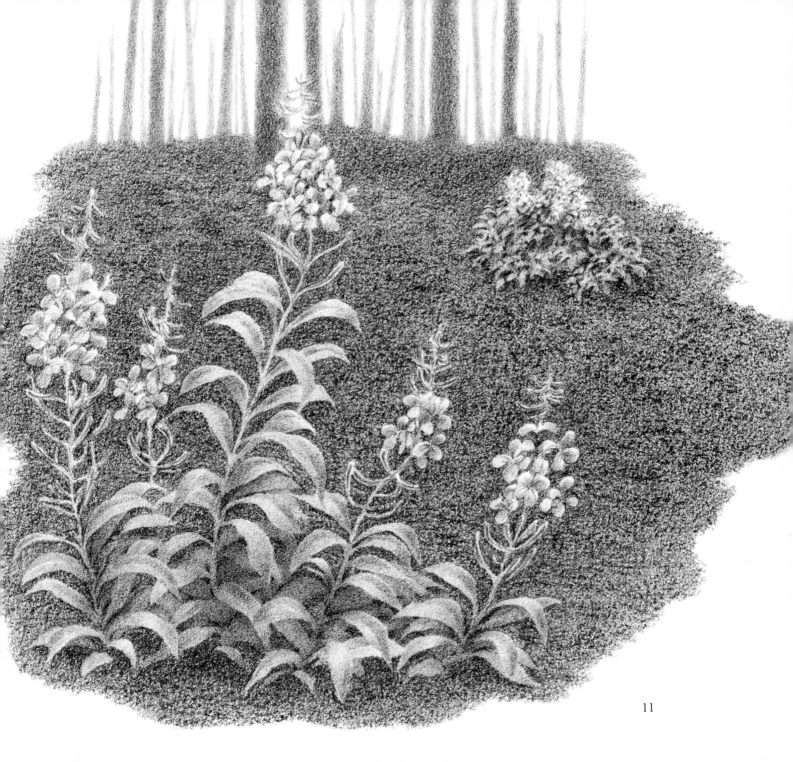

Coyote

Brush rabbit

Soon, animals begin to return. Rabbits nibble on the fresh green blades of grass. Coyotes come back to hunt the rabbits.

Birds crisscross the damaged land feeding on the insects that are gathering nectar from the new flowers.

Oregon junco

14

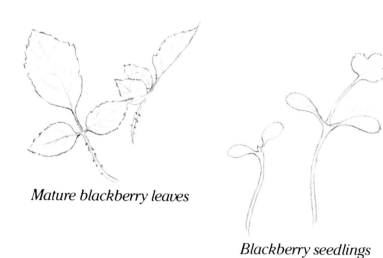

Mature blackberry leaves

Blackberry seedlings

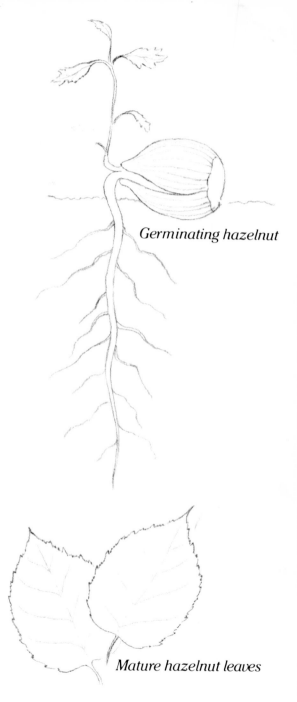

Germinating hazelnut

Before the first year has passed, other plants begin to grow in the shade of the grasses and flowers. These plants need shade only during the first part of their lives. Some of them, like the blackberry bushes, push up from roots that had stayed alive underground during the fire. Hazelnuts that had survived the heat and flames in the litter of the forest floor start to germinate.

Mature hazelnut leaves

15

Huckleberry, serviceberry, and other bushes begin
to grow when their seeds are dropped by birds.

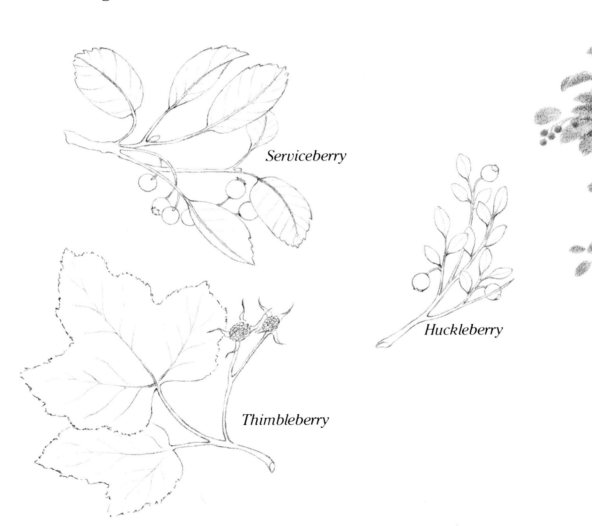

Serviceberry

Huckleberry

Thimbleberry

Ruffed grouse

Douglas squirrel

Raccoon

Squirrels, raccoons, and grouse come to the bushes
to feed on berries and nuts.

17

Lodgepole pine seedlings

18

As these bushes grow they shade the sun-loving plants beneath them. Because they no longer have the sunlight they need, the grasses and flowers begin to die.

Small trees appear in the shade of the bushes and burned stumps. One kind, the lodgepole pine, owes its new life to the forest fire. Without the heat of the blaze, many of the sticky cones from the parent lodgepole pines might never have opened to release their seeds.

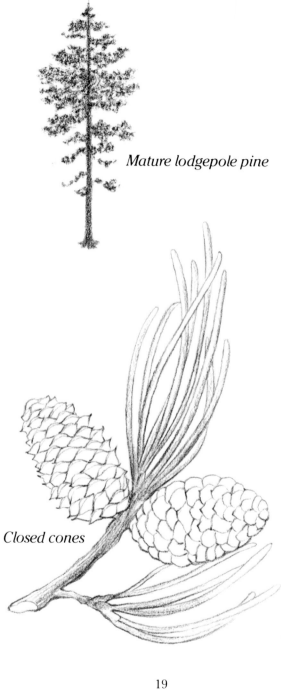

Mature lodgepole pine

Closed cones

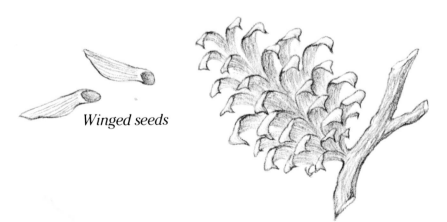

Winged seeds

Open cone

19

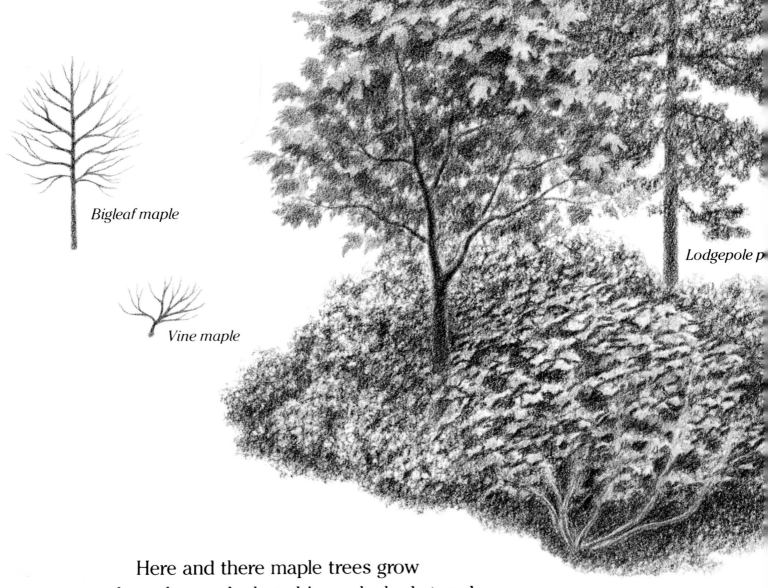

Bigleaf maple

Vine maple

Lodgepole p

Here and there maple trees grow
from the seeds that chipmunks had stored
underground before the fire.

Deer browse on the tender
new shoots of alder saplings.

Red alder saplings

Black-tailed deer

Spruce seedlings

After many years these fast-growing trees grow enough to keep most of the sunlight from reaching the bushes. The bushes begin to die in the shade of the small trees.

As the bushes disappear they are replaced by seedlings of hemlock and spruce. With the help of the wind, their seeds had been sprinkled into the burned-over area. These will be the forest giants. Someday, in a century or more, they will tower above the smaller trees and shade them out.

Hemlock seedlings

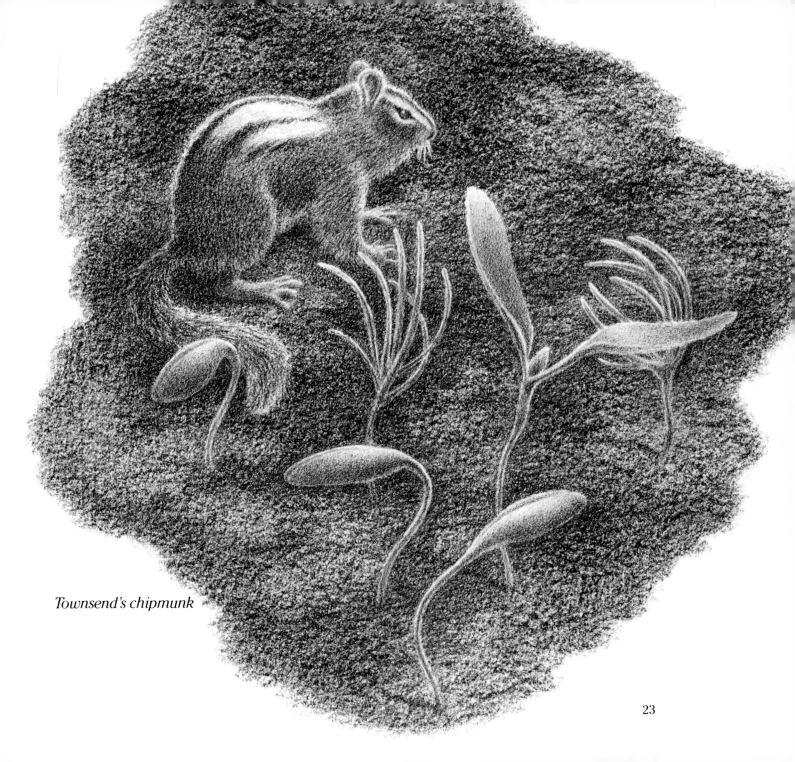

Townsend's chipmunk

23

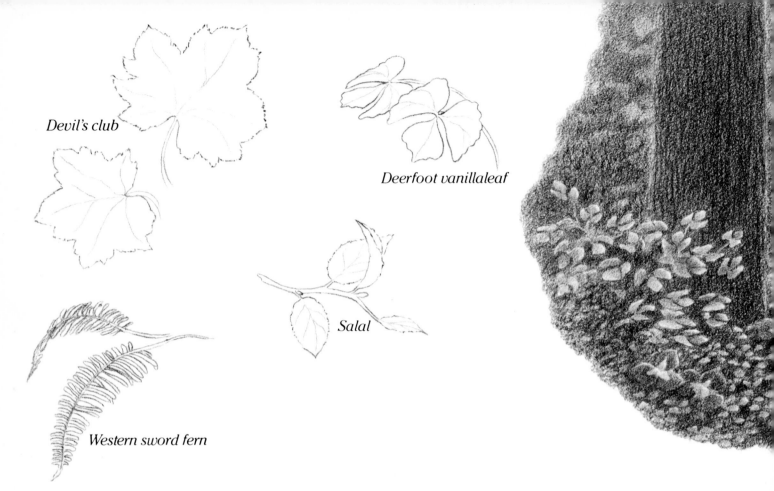

Devil's club

Deerfoot vanillaleaf

Salal

Western sword fern

Many of the smaller trees will be replaced
by sword ferns, vanillaleaf, salal, and other plants
that can live in the deep shade of the forest.
Their large leaves will catch the few rays of
sunlight that filter down through the roof
of tree branches.

Wood lily

24

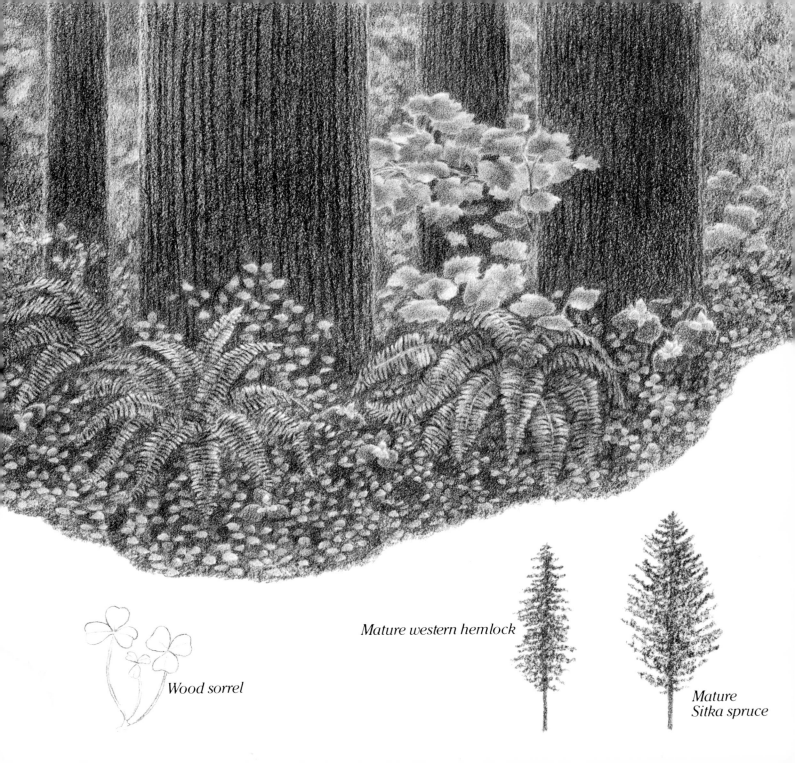

Wood sorrel

Mature western hemlock

Mature Sitka spruce

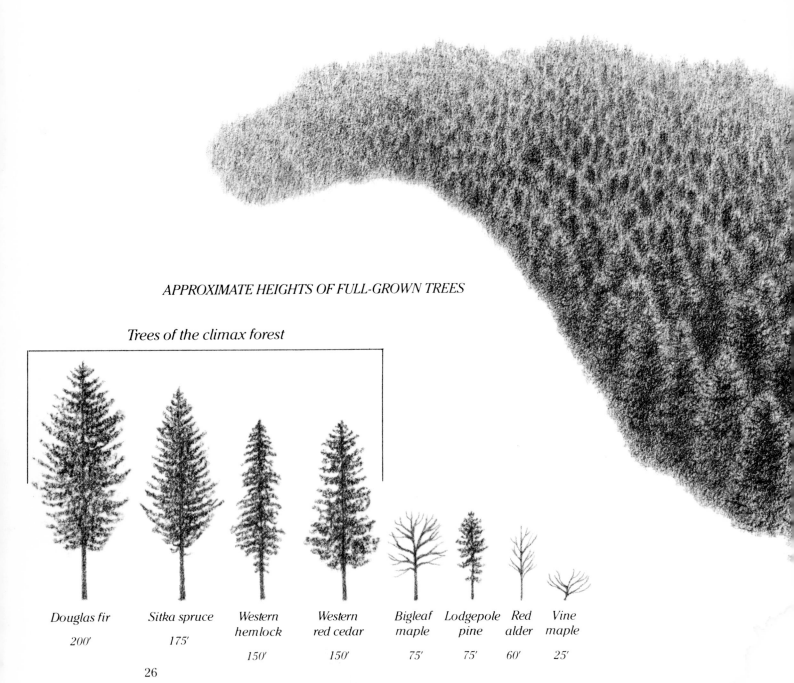

APPROXIMATE HEIGHTS OF FULL-GROWN TREES

Trees of the climax forest

Douglas fir	Sitka spruce	Western hemlock	Western red cedar	Bigleaf maple	Lodgepole pine	Red alder	Vine maple
200'	175'	150'	150'	75'	75'	60'	25'

This will be a full-grown, or climax, forest.
It will be made up of the kinds of plants that are
best suited to grow in its particular soil
and climate.

This climax forest will stay much the same
until something major happens to change it.
Floods, droughts, logging, and even volcanic eruptions
have altered countless climax forests. The change
may come by the trees falling prey to great numbers
of wood-damaging insects. Perhaps some person may
become careless with fire. Or, once again,
lightning may provide the sparks that set
the forest ablaze.

Author's Note

*While the setting for this story is on a western slope
of the Cascade Range in the Pacific Northwest, the
renewal of a forest is much the same throughout
the world. Wherever land is laid bare, an orderly
succession of plants and animals native to the area
will occur.*